THE **ADVENTURES** OF
BILLY
AND THE
BIG-EARS
GANG

Robert Nuttall

authorHOUSE

AuthorHouse™ UK
1663 Liberty Drive
Bloomington, IN 47403 USA
www.authorhouse.co.uk
Phone: UK TFN: 0800 0148641 (Toll Free inside the UK)
*   UK Local: (02) 0369 56322 (+44 20 3695 6322 from outside the UK)*

Published by AuthorHouse 07/22/2024

ISBN: 979-8-8230-8842-8 (sc)
ISBN: 979-8-8230-8844-2 (hc)
ISBN: 979-8-8230-8843-5 (e)

Library of Congress Control Number: 2024912929

Print information available on the last page.

This book is printed on acid-free paper.

ACKNOWLEDGMENT

These three bedtime stories are for my beautiful granddaughter Sienna Milly. Sienna lives in London with her mummy and daddy, Lucy, Guy and Pablo, their dog.

PROLOGUE

Billy Nuts

Billy Nuts is a wheaten terrier; he's ten years old and is a white long-haired dog with long ears. He often looks untidy because of his hairy coat, but he's a very kind dog and loves cuddles. He's a clever dog, but he does have silly spells—usually when his cousin Pablo comes to visit on his holidays.

He lives with his human mum and dad (Pablos's grandpa and grandma). He loves going on the local heath for his walks; it's exciting because it's surrounded by woods, and there are lots of rabbits, squirrels, and deer living there.

Pablo

Pablo is a small French bulldog; at two years old, he is still a puppy, really. He is light and dark brown with big ears that stand upright. His main goals in life are having lots of fun, eating, getting Billy to chase him, eating lots more, and getting Billy to chase him again. He gets in to trouble a lot, because he can be very naughty. He eats Billy's food when Billy isn't looking.

He sees his reflection in a mirror or a glass door and thinks it's another dog, and he stalks the reflection and begins barking, trying to pick a fight with himself. He's really frightened of his own shadow, but when Billy is next to him, he suddenly becomes very brave. He also doesn't like people looking at him; he barks at them.

This happens a lot because he is so cute. He's also very nosey. He loves summer because he likes nothing better than to relax in the garden and sunbathe. Pablo is Billy's cousin, and he comes to stay with him for his holidays; he loves it at Billy's. For one thing, he gets lots of treats—more than he does at home, but don't tell his mummy and daddy.

Charlie

Charlie is a brown and ginger Labradoodle, with long hair and long, droopy, fluffy ears. He's four years old, and he's a nice dog. But unfortunately, he behaves like a grumpy old man. He's always complaining about anything and everything, but most of all, he complains about Pablo. Charlie lives around the corner and goes on walks with Billy; he doesn't like it when Pablo is there.

He thinks Pablo is a silly boy who talks too much; he gives Charlie a headache. They are not really a gang; they only agreed to that to stop Pablo from going on and on that they should be a gang. They also let him decide the name of the gang. He thought long and hard for a day, so much that it gave him a headache. He finally came up with the name Billy and the Big-Ear Gang. Billy secretly thought it was a good name for the gang.

PABLO'S
BIG SECRET

It was a sunny morning in summer, and Pablo had come to stay at Billy's the evening before for his two-week holiday.

That meant lots of fun outside and lots of exciting things to do with his cousin Billy. Also, hopefully there would be lots of yummy treats, and he would probably get into trouble doing naughty things.

Billy liked to take his time eating his food but Pablo would rush his food' then sit next to Billy.

When Billy looked away Pablo would take his treat and run off into the bushes and eat it.

The best thing was Billy didn't mind; he really was the best cousin ever in Pablo's eyes. Pablo slept on the sofa in the kitchen; Billy slept upstairs on his owner's bed. Pablo wasn't allowed because he got too excited, and when he finally went to sleep, he snored very loudly. That morning he had already eaten his breakfast and was waiting for Billy to get up so they could start playing.

He was out in the garden having a wee and sniffing around the bushes when he found a hole in the fence.

The hole was behind a big green bush; you couldn't see it from the house, and Grandpa probably didn't know it was there. It was Pablo's secret. He had never had a secret before, and he couldn't wait for Billy to get up so he could share his very first big secret with him.

Billy finally came down into the kitchen, and Pablo ran in from the garden to say good morning.

He sat next to Billy, who was eating his breakfast. If Grandpa saw him, he would get in to trouble.

But Billy didn't mind, and sometimes he would save a little food in his bowl for Pablo.

It didn't matter if he didn't. When Billy had finished, Pablo would always lick all around the bowl anyway.

Billy finished and went outside for a wee, and Pablo came flying out and waited for Billy to finish.

He whispered, "Billy, come on; follow me. I've got something to show you, but you mustn't tell anyone. It's our secret."

Billy tutted and followed his excited cousin down the garden, thinking it was probably nothing. Pablo got excited about the smallest things.

Billy followed him behind the green bush and stopped behind Pablo, who was looking at the fence.

Pablo said, "Look, Billy; what do you think?"

Billy said, "What are we supposed to be looking at?" Pablo said, "This!"

Billy replied, "It's a hole in the fence; is that your secret?"

Pablo said excitedly, "Yes! Nobody knows about it except us. We can get out and go on adventures, without Grandpa and Grandy knowing. If they can't see us, they will just think we are in the other garden at the back of the garages."

Billy looked from Pablo back to the hole and eventually said, "Umm, you know we are not supposed to go out on our own; we could get in lots of trouble if they found out."

Pablo laughed and replied, "But you've got to admit it is exciting, having our very own secret hole in the garden fence. Also, we can go on the heath on our own and have fun and get other dogs to chase us and play ball."

Billy smiled and said, "Yes, I suppose it is pretty cool." And with that, he popped his head through the hole.

Pablo shouted excitedly, "What can you see, Billy? Can I have a look?"

Billy replied, "Nothing, really—just grass."

Pablo impatiently said, "Can I see, Billy? Can I see, please?" And before Billy could pull his head out, Pablo stuck his head through the hole next to him.

Billy puffed and screwed up his nose and said, "Pablo, there isn't enough room for both of us, you silly boy. Take get your head out."

Pablo moved back and twisted his head left and then right; then he finally stopped wriggling and said, "I can't get my head out. I think we're stuck, Billy. Can you get your head out?"

Billy said, "Your head is smaller than mine; if you can't get out, I certain can't." But he did move backwards slightly and tried to free his head.

Pablo yelped and said, "Billy, you're squashing me; you've pulled my ears off! Ouch!"

"Don't be so silly," Billy replied. "Your ears won't come off; they're not screwed on."

Pablo said, "Pardon? I can't hear you." Then he laughed loudly; he thought his little joke was funny. "Well, it felt like they were going to come off. I'm sure something's come off. Maybe it was just one of my ears. Oh no, did one of them fall off? Can you look for it, Billy?"

Billy could only move his head a little without Pablo complaining, but he looked to his left and said, "You're okay, Pablo; you've still got both ears on top of your head."

They both stood there in silence for a few minutes, thinking about what they could do. Billy was starting to get hot. Pablo was just hoping he still had his big ears on top of his head.

Pablo announced, "My back leg is itchy. Can you scratch it for me?"

Billy tutted. "How can I do that when we are both stuck in the fence and can't move?"

"Only our heads are stuck, Billy. If you lift your back leg a little, you will be able to scratch my itch."

Billy tutted again and let out a big sigh. "This is ridiculous. Who gets their heads stuck in a hole?" With that he raised his left leg and rubbed Pablo's hairy little leg.

Pablo shouted, "Ouch! You just kicked me, Billy; that's not very nice. I couldn't help getting our heads stuck. You've got to admit it is quite funny, isn't it?" And with that, he started to laugh again.

"It's not funny, Pablo. I think we will have to get Grandpa to come and rescue us; otherwise we will be stuck here forever."

Pablo looked worried. "Do you think Grandpa will be annoyed and think we made the hole in his fence?"

Billy replied, "No, he won't think we made the hole." With that they both started barking loudly, but Pablo kept stopping to laugh. He thought it was very funny; he had never had his head stuck anywhere before.

After a minute or two, they heard Grandpa shouting their names. Then they heard him behind them. "What have you two done? How have you got your heads stuck in the fence?"

Before Billy could speak, Pablo fibbed.

"We were running so fast that we couldn't

stop, and we smashed right through the

fence—didn't we, Billy?"

Billy whispered, "Silly, he's not going to

believe that!"

Grandpa fetched a pair of cutters and

gently cut away some of the fence to make

the hole bigger.

Billy backed out and shook his head, followed by Pablo, who said, "Thanks, Grandpa! You saved my life. I could have died in there."

Grandpa smiled and replied, "I don't think so, little man. I will get a new piece of fencing. Billy, you and Pablo stay away from that hole, okay?"

Pablo said, "Grandpa, have I lost an ear? Are they all still there?"

Grandpa replied, "No, they are still on top of your head, little man; why do you ask?"

Pablo said "Billy moved, and it felt like my ear fell off. When I asked him, he said I still had both. What does *both* mean, Grandpa? Does that mean I've lost one?"

Grandpa laughed. "No, it doesn't, Pablo; you still have two ears. *Both* is another way of saying *two*; that's all."

Pablo was relieved. "Oh, so that is what it means. Thanks, Grandpa. I'm glad I haven't lost one. I wouldn't want to go to the vet to have it fixed back on."

Pablo didn't like going to the vet; they would give him treats and then sneakily try to give him tablets or medicine.

Billy and Pablo walked back into the kitchen to have a drink of water. They then both sat down on the cool kitchen floor tiles to relax out of the sun. Pablo looked at Billy and said, "It was good having a secret, wasn't it, Billy? We should get another one soon."

THE DRAGON ON THE HEATH

Billy and Pablo went for a walk on the heath near their home with Grandpa, and they called for Charlie. They always looked forward to the walks. Pablo loved the heath because it involved lots of chasing. He loved being chased, even by other dogs. They would chase him, but he was too fast for them.

The more excited Pablo got, the more he would talk, and this annoyed Charlie, who told Pablo to be quiet and then would sulk and walk behind.

On the heath they were having fun running around and chasing each other, and even grumpy Charlie joined in. Because it was warm, they went into the woods; it was cooler in the shade of the tall trees.

Also, there was lots of scents that they could smell, and as usual, Pablo wandered off following a scent of a squirrel. He didn't realise that he was on his own as he followed the trail. He was sniffing away when he heard a loud snort from behind two tall trees.

He didn't pay too much attention, but then he heard it again—and this time it was closer and louder. Curious, Pablo popped his head around the tree and got the fright of his life. He saw a long pair of legs. He looked higher and saw a large head with big flaring nostrils. It was a dragon, and it breathed a burst of fire into the air.

Pablo yelped and jumped back; he ran has fast has his little legs would carry him. He ran through a big bush. He yelped again and ran into Billy; then he looked up and saw Billy looking down at him.

"What's wrong?" Billy asked. "I heard you scream and came to help."

Pablo shouted, "Quick, Billy, run for your life—there's a dragon chasing me! He's trying to fry me with fire from his mouth."

Billy heard a noise in the woods behind Pablo and said very quietly, "Shush, Pablo. There is something there; keep quiet, and it might not see us. We can't outrun a dragon."

"I bet we could. I'm scared," said Pablo, shaking and getting closer and closer to Billy. He was underneath Billy's tummy now with his head peering out.

Billy said, "Shush, it's very close now."

They could hear the noise getting closer and closer; it was over the other side of some trees. Billy was worried, but he been on the heath lots and had never seen a dragon. He looked up and saw a huge snorting head; it was a horse with a lady rider. She said hello to Billy.

Billy looked down at Pablo; his eyes were closed, and he was shaking. Billy stepped back and said "Pablo!"

With his eyes still closed, Pablo said, "Is it going to eat us, Billy? Is this the end?"

Billy laughed and replied, "I doubt it, silly. Horses don't eat dogs; they eat hay."

Pablo slowly opened his eyes and said, "Horses—what are they?"

Billy said, "Well, for a start, they are not dragons, and they don't beath fire either, you silly boy!"

Pablo stood up and looked down the path; he saw the back of the big horse walking away. He said, "I've never seen a horse up close before; I thought it was a dragon. I saw a picture of one in baby Sienna's book; it looked just like that horse."

Billy smiled and said, "I don't think so, Pablo, and it certainly wouldn't have breathed fire at you. I think you were frightened and just thought it was a dragon."

Pablo said, "I think you're right, Billy. I nearly overreacted there, didn't I?"

THE ROBBERY

Billy and Pablo were sat in the garden sunbathing when Pablo announced, "I'm bored, Billy. What can we do?"

Billy sighed and replied, "How can you be bored we've just had breakfast?"

Pablo lifted his head and sniffed the air. Then he asked, "What's that yummy smell?"

Billy said, "It's Grandpa cooking sausages for breakfast. He gets them from Mr Chapman, the butcher in the village."

Pablo said, "Do you think he will share them with us?"

Billy said, "No, for two reasons. One, we've just had our breakfast, and two, he puts mustard on them. They would be too hot for us to eat. He did let me have some once, though; it was the best thing I've ever tasted."

Pablo said, "Well, why don't we go and buy some just for us? We know where the shop is. We've had to stand outside on our walks while Grandpa bought meat."

Billy replied, "How can we? We don't have any money, and we are not allowed in the shop, because we are dogs."

Pablo smiled and said, "I know, but we could sneak in and just borrow some sausages. I've noticed if Mr Chapman isn't serving, sometimes he goes into the back of the shop."

Billy was shocked. "But that's stealing, Pablo. If we get caught, we could be in big trouble!"

Pablo said, "No, not for stealing three sausages. We can get Charlie to stand across the road in the bus shelter and look out for Mr Chapman."

Billy thought about it. Even though it was wrong, he did like sausages. He remembered the taste when Grandpa had given him some that day; it was very, very yummy. Much against his better judgement, he agreed to Pablos's naughty plan.

Early the next morning after breakfast, Billy and Pablo left Grandpa in the kitchen and went to the side gate. Pablo jumped up onto Billy's back and undid the latch with his teeth, and then they ran down the drive. After picking up Charlie on the way, they went to the parade of shops on the high street. Charlie went across the road and sat in the bus shelter, with a clear view of Mr Chapman's shop. Billy and Pablo sat outside the coffee shop two doors down, and on Charlie's bark, they ran into the butcher's shop. Billy stood against the counter, and Pablo jumped up on his back.

Seeing the tray of juicy sausages, he went to grab them. But his nose squashed against the glass protecting the meat. They had never actually been in to the shop, so they didn't know there was glass below the counter where the customers stood.

Suddenly, they heard a loud voice shout,

"Hey! What are you two doing in here?"

It was Mr Chapman, who had come back

into his shop. Billy and Pablo looked up at

him and in fright ran out of the shop as fast

as they could.

Hiding on the pavement next to the post

office, Billy peeped around the corner to

see whether Mr Chapman was chasing

them. Pablo asked breathlessly, "Can you

see him, Billy?"

Billy shook his head and said, "No, he's not there, but neither is Charlie at the bus stop across the road. He was supposed to warn us if Mr Chapman came back into the shop."

Pablo said, "I think it's best we go home now before we get into more trouble." They were walking along when the saw Charlie running up the road towards them.

Charlie looked at them both and asked, "Where are the sausages? You haven't eaten mine, have you?"

Billy explained what had happened and asked why he didn't warn them that Mr Chapman came back.

Charlie said, "A bus came, and an old lady got on board. Then the driver looked at me and said, 'Well, come on; we haven't got all day.' When he realised, I wasn't with the old lady, he made me get off at the next stop."

Billy and Pablo started laughing, and to their surprise, grumpy Charlie also started laughing very loudly.

The three friends started off back home. Pablo said, "I'm glad we didn't get the sausages, because that would have been wrong and very naughty." Billy and Charlie both agreed; it had all turned out for the best.

When Billy and Pablo got home, Grandpa came out into the garden and said, "I was just coming out to get you two. Come with me; I've got a treat for you both for being good boys."

They followed him into the kitchen, and in their bowls were two fat cooked sausages. So they hadn't done anything naughty that sunny day, and they still got yummy sausages to eat after all.